characters created by
lauren child

whoOps!
But it wasn't
me

PUFFIN

Text based on script written by

Bridget Hurst and Carol Noble

Illustrations from the TV animation

produced by Tiger Aspect

PUFFIN BOOKS
Published by the Penguin Group: London, New York, Australia,
Canada, India, Ireland, New Zealand and South Africa
Penguin Books Ltd, Registered Offices: 80 Strand, London WC2R 0RL, England

puffinbooks.com

First published in Puffin Books 2006
This edition published 2012
001 – 10 9 8 7 6 5 4 3 2 1
Text and illustrations copyright © Lauren Child/Tiger Aspect Productions Limited, 2006
Charlie and Lola word and logo ® and © Lauren Child, 2005
Charlie and Lola is produced by Tiger Aspect Productions
All rights reserved
The moral right of the author/illustrator has been asserted
Made and printed in China
ISBN (pack): 978-0-718-19386-7

I have this little sister Lola.
    She is small and very funny.
Sometimes Lola likes to play
          with my things.
    Usually I don't mind.

One day I come home from school
with the best thing I have ever made.

Lola says, "Ooooh!"

I say,
"It took me ten days,
    three hours and forty minutes
to make the outside,
        which is called
the superstructure...

"... It's built from three cereal packets,

ten yoghurt pots,

28 bottle tops,

157 sweet wrappers

and a roll of extra-wide tinfoil."

Lola says, "Ooooh!"

I say, "Don't **touch** it!
This rocket is **really** breakable.
I don't mind you playing with
most of my things,
but you must **double**,
triple promise
you'll **NEVER** play
with it."

"Let's play something
        else then," says Lola.
    I say, "I've promised to play football
        with Marv."
"But what am I going to do?" says Lola.
        And I say, "Why don't you play
    with Soren Lorensen?"

Soren Lorensen is Lola's imaginary friend.
No one can see him except for Lola.

And Lola says,
    "Soren Lorensen always wants
to play with me."

"Hello, Soren Lorensen," says Lola.
"Charlie's gone to play football with Marv,
so we can play a very good game,
        can't we?"

And Soren Lorensen says,
        "Yes, with those two hyenas
that are brothers and twins and
        that tiny small elephant."

Lola says, "Oh yes, Ellie.

"Where will the adventure be?"

Soren Lorensen says,
"The place where all the animals live."

And Lola says,
"In Animal Land."

Soren Lorensen says, "Ellie is really sad because
he doesn't like the nasty hyenas
laughing at him."

"Those **hyenas** are **meanies**, aren't they?" says Lola.
"What are we going to do?"

"We can't leave Ellie all sad," says Lola.
"He must go back to all his nice friends in Animal Land...
but how are we going to get him there?"

Then Soren Lorensen points to the rocket.

Lola says,
"But that is an extremely breakable and special rocket
and Charlie said that we should never,
NEVER touch it or play with it."

"But I think what Charlie meant was that if
we did play with it, we must be extra
specially careful," says Soren Lorensen.

So Lola reaches up to get the rocket.

Soren Lorensen says,
   "Remember to be extra
specially careful, Lola."

And Lola says,

"I am!
I am!"

Then she says,

"Oh no!"

Lola looks at the pieces of broken rocket.
"You know, I think that when
things are broken they can always be
mended and made like new..."

"If we both act normally, Lola,
then Charlie might not think
we did it," says Soren Lorensen.

Lola whispers,
"No, he'll never know."

When I get home I shout,
"My rocket!
Lola!
Did you break
my rocket?"

Lola says,
"I didn't break your
rocket, Charlie."

I say,
"You are telling a big lie, Lola!
And you know it!"

"Don't tell Mum!"
says Lola. "Wait, Charlie!
I just have to quickly talk
to Soren Lorensen."

Lola says, "Do you think we should tell him
what really happened?"
Soren Lorensen says, "Maybe we could tell Charlie
somebody else broke the rocket?"
And Lola says, "Yes! Because it is nearly true!"

So Lola comes to talk to me.
"Charlie, Soren Lorensen and me have got something
      very **extremely** important to tell you."

I say, "What?"

Lola says,
"It is the real **true** story of who **broke**
      your special **rocket**.

"Well, me and Soren Lorensen were **playing** in our room, Charlie, and Ellie needed to go in your **rocket**.

I didn't think it was a good idea, but he **had** to get away.

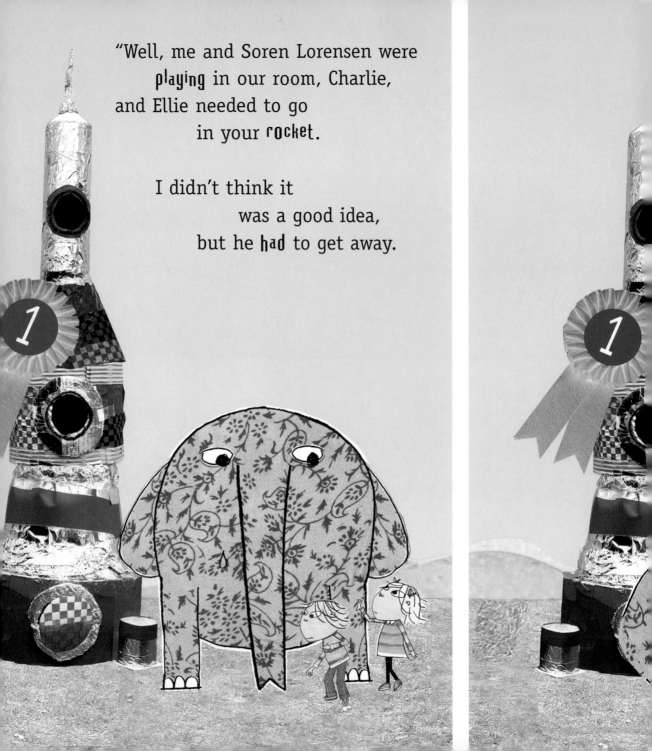

So we **squeezed**
Ellie, and it was
a real **squish**.
But we **did** it.

And then we **took off**.

Whoosh! Whoosh!

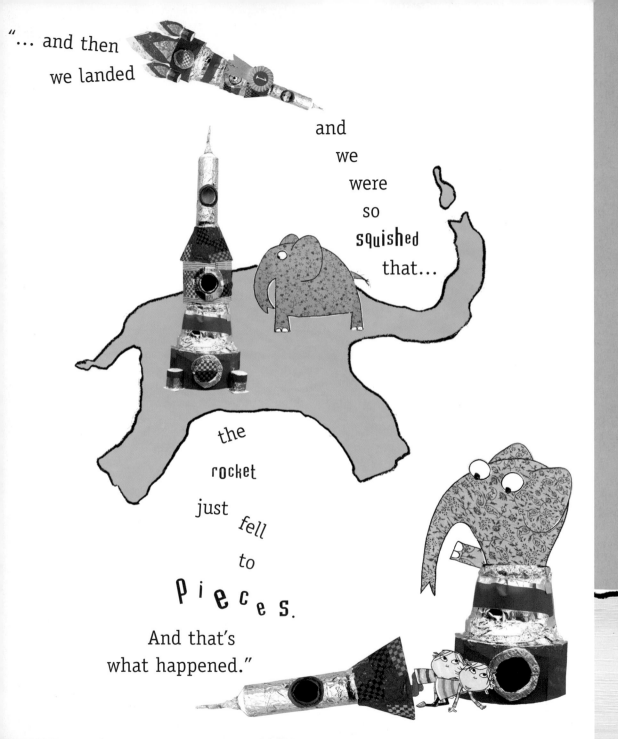

"... and then
we landed
and
we
were
so
squished
that...

the
rocket
just fell
to
Pieces.
And that's
what happened."

I say,

"Right.
I'm going to
tell Mum!"

"Oh dear, I don't think he
believed us," says Soren Lorensen.

Lola says,
"I think I have to tell
Charlie the truth. But will it
make Charlie like me again?"

Soren Lorensen says,
"As long as you say sorry too."

Lola knocks at the door.
"Soren Lorensen
really wants to say sorry
for breaking your
rocket, Charlie."

So I just shut
the door.

Then there's another knock
and Lola says,
 "It was me that broke
your rocket. Just as I was
 getting your extremely
special rocket down from
the really high shelf...
 it fell and broke
 into lots
 of pieces.

I am really ever so sorry
 for breaking your
extremely special rocket,
 Charlie."

And I say,
"Are you **really**, Lola?"

Lola says, "**Sorry**, Charlie."

And she does look really very sorry.

So I say, "That's OK.
At least you've told the **truth**."

Then Lola sees the rocket.

"You **mended** it, Charlie!" she says.

And I say,
"Yes, Lola, I've **mended** it."

"I like it," says Lola.
I say,
"Don't touch it!"